The Selfish Giant

Sky Pony Press books may be purchased in bulk at special discounts for sales promotion, corporate gifts, fund-raising, or educational purposes. Special editions can also be created to specifications. For details, contact the Special Sales Department, Sky Pony Press, 307 West 36th Street, 11th Floor, New York, NY 10018 or info@skyhorsepublishing.com.

Sky Pony® is a registered trademark of Skyhorse Publishing, Inc.®, a Delaware corporation.

Visit our website at www.skyponypress.com.

10 9 8 7 6 5 4 3 2 1

Manufactured in China, April 2015
This product conforms to CPSIA 2008

Library of Congress Cataloging-in-Publication Data is available on file.

Cover illustration credit: Bill Bell

ISBN: 978-1-5107-0306-3
Ebook ISBN: 978-0-06192-453-8

Oscar Wilde's

The Selfish Giant

Retold by Mary Hollingsworth

Illustrations by Bill Bell

Sky Pony Press
New York

Dear Reader

The story of *The Selfish Giant*
reveals another side of its author, Oscar Wilde,
who is more often identified with wit and sophistication.
Here, his story is wistful, sentimental, mystical, spiritual.
It's an interesting tale that I enjoyed
illustrating. I hope you will enjoy
a visit with the Selfish Giant.

Bill Bell

"Those whom the gods love grow young."—Oscar Wilde

Once upon a wondrous time in a happy other land was a beautiful garden. Now, this was no ordinary garden. It belonged to a Giant who had been away a very long time.

Every day, children came to the wonderful garden and danced in the gentle breeze. Here and there flowers poked their heads up through the grass, like stars, birds sang, and the children ran and played.

Around the edge of the garden grew twelve peach trees. In Spring, the trees burst into pretty blossoms of pink and pearl. In Autumn, the trees gave the children sweet, juicy peaches to eat. The children were very happy in the garden.

Then the Giant came home. He had been staying with his friend, the Cornish ogre. But after seven years, they had nothing left to say. So, the Giant decided to return to his own castle. When he arrived, he found the children playing in his garden.

"What are you doing here?" growled the Giant in a very gruff voice. "This is my garden. I will not let anyone play here but me." He was a very selfish Giant.

The children were afraid and ran away. At once, the Giant built a high wall around his garden and put a big sign across the gate that read:

TRESPASSERS
WILL BE PROSECUTED!

The children knew the sign meant they could no longer play in the garden. "Where will we play now" they asked each other.

The only place to play was
on the dusty road. But the road
was full of rocks and stones that
hurt their feet. It was no fun to
play in the road.

Every day the children walked
by the high wall around the garden.
Sometimes they lifted each other
up and peaked inside. They had
been so happy in the garden.

Winter came and went. Then it was Spring. All over the country the trees were blooming, and the birds were singing. But in the Giant's garden, it was still Winter!

The trees in the garden refused to bloom. The birds no longer came to sing. All because they missed the children. Once a beautiful flower poked its head up through the frozen ground. But when it saw the Giant's ugly sign, it felt so sad for the children that it tucked its head back under the snowy cover and went back to sleep.

now and Frost laughed and said, "Spring has forgotten this garden; so we can live here all year 'round!"

Snow covered the grass with her great white blanket. Frost painted all the peach trees an icy silver. Then they invited North Wind, who arrived bundled up in his warm, winter hat and mittens. He raced around the garden all day long, roaring and blowing.

"This is a wonderful place!" cried North Wind. "Let's ask our friend Hail to come for a visit, too."

Hail came dressed in cloudy gray. He played chase with North Wind. And when he laughed, his breath fell like tiny ice droplets that beat down on the castle and broke the Giant's roof.

The selfish Giant sat at his window and looked out at his cold, white garden. I wonder why Spring is so late this year? he thought. I hope the weather changes soon.

Sadly, Spring never came, nor did Summer. And Autumn brought no peaches.

"The Giant is just too selfish," said Autumn. "He would not share the peaches with the children."

So, it was always Winter in the garden. North Wind, Hail, Frost, and Snow frolicked and danced about the trees with delight.

Early one morning, the
Giant was lying awake shiver-
ing in his large bed. He pulled
his huge downy covers up to his
chin. Suddenly, he heard music so
sweet that he thought it must be
the King's band marching outside.
But it was a little bird singing
outside in his garden. He thought
it was the most beautiful song in
the world!

Then Hail stopped tapping on
the roof. North Wind quit his rac-
ing and roaring. Snow and Frost
jumped over the garden wall and
ran far, far away.

"I do believe Spring has finally
come!" grinned the Giant. And he
threw back the covers and looked
outside.

To his amazement, children were everywhere! They had come in through a hole in the wall. They were sitting in the branches of the trees. This made the trees so happy that they had at once burst into full bloom and were waving their branches gently above the children's heads to keep them cool.

The birds were twittering. The squirrels were playing tag with rabbits. And the flowers had all poked out their colorful heads to watch.

The Giant stuck his big, hairy head out the window to look at the pretty scene. Spring was everywhere . . . well, almost everywhere. Curiously, in one corner of the garden, it was still Winter!

North Wind still raced around one peach tree. Wandering under its frosty limbs was a little boy. He was crying because he was too small to reach the tree's branches and climb up.

"Climb up, little boy!" begged the Tree. And it bent its branches down as low as it could to help. But the little boy was just too tiny.

The Giant's heart melted as he watched. "How selfish I've been," he said. "Now I know why Spring wouldn't come here." He was really so sorry for what he had done.

So the Giant crept down the stairs, opened the big front door quite softly, and went out into the garden. When the children saw him, they were afraid and ran away. As they left, Winter came hurrying back.

Only the little boy in the far corner did not run. The boy's eyes were so full of tears that he didn't see the Giant coming. The Giant took the tiny boy gently in his huge hands and lifted him into the tree.

Instantly, the tree burst into blossoms and birds flew to its branches singing. The little boy reached out his two tiny arms and wrapped them as far as he could around the Giant's big neck and kissed him.

When the other children saw that the Giant was no longer angry, they ran back to the garden. And with them came Spring.

"It's your garden now, my little friends," said the Giant. Then he took a large hammer and knocked down the wall around the garden.

After that, the children came to play with the gentle Giant in his special garden.

Every day the Giant asked the children, "Where is your little friend? The one I put into the tree?" The Giant loved him best because he had kissed him.

"We don't know," said the children. "He has gone away. We had never seen him before."

The Giant felt very sad.

The Giant was very kind to the children. Still, he wished for his first little friend to come, and he often talked about him to the other children. "I surely would like to see him," he would say.

Many years went by, and the Giant grew old and weak. When he could no longer play with the children, he sat on a huge chair and watched their games. Sometimes he told them giant stories. And, often, he smiled at his beautiful garden.

I have many beautiful flowers, he thought, but the children are the most beautiful flowers of all. This garden shall always belong to the children.

One winter morning, the Giant looked out his window and rubbed his eyes in disbelief. The tree where he had helped the little boy was covered with lovely white blossoms. Silver peaches hung down from its golden branches. And underneath it was the little boy he had so loved.

J oyfully, the Giant raced downstairs into the garden. But when he got close to the boy, he became so angry that his face turned red.

"Who has dared to hurt you?" he asked. For he could see the prints of two nails in the child's hands and the prints of two nails on his tiny feet. "Tell me, and I will take my sword to him."

"No!" said the child. "These wounds show how much I love you."

"Who are you?" asked the Giant, as a wonderful feeling came over him. Then he slowly knelt before the child.

The child smiled sweetly at the gentle Giant and again kissed him. "You once let me play in your wonderful garden. Today, you shall come with me to my garden, which is called Paradise."

That afternoon when the children came, they found the Giant under the tree. He had died there with a smile on his face and white blossoms gently covering him.